THE LAST DEAF CLUB
IN AMERICA

THE LAST DEAF CLUB IN AMERICA

Raymond Luczak

Handtype Press
Minneapolis, MN

in gratitude

The author thanks Bex Freund, Lilah Katcher, Rachel C. Mazique, Jeremy Quiroga, and Cynthia Weitzel for their support while writing this story's first draft as part of the Deaf Artist Residency Program at the Anderson Center for Interdisciplinary Arts in Red Wing, Minnesota. He is equally grateful to Anthony Santos and Tom Steele for their continued support over the years. Much appreciation goes to Andrew J. Oehrlein for his historical clarifications, and to John Lee Clark and David Cummer for their editorial insights.

notice

copyright

"As long as we have deaf people on earth, we will have signs. And as long as we have our films, we can preserve signs in their old purity. It is my hope that we will all love and guard our beautiful sign language as the noblest gift God has given to deaf people."

—George Veditz, 1913

for Cynthia Weitzel

A NOTE ON THE TEXT

ɔrmed reader may notice the seemingly variable spelling in the word "deaf" throughout the text.

In Deaf culture, the capital-D "Deaf" refers to those with hearing loss who communicate primarily through Sign and associate with each other. ~~This was~~

Those who are "deaf" tend to identify themselves with hearing people and think of their hearing loss in medical terms.

THE MEETING

Ghosts are everywhere. Their breaths, drained of blood, seep through cracks of the places they choose to haunt. They become oxygen that go into the lungs of those still alive. For a few seconds they feel warm and human. This is why they linger.

Yet they cannot be seen with the human eye; only felt with a whisper of chill on the neck and maybe with a light tap on the shoulder. Their sorrowful presence becomes heavier than lead. Elders older than time itself say that what ghosts see of each other are only mirrors of their physical selves the last moment before they died, but without none of the baggage associated with physicality. Only their faces and hands are imbued with ghostlight.

Ghosts are renowned for their language of unfinished longing, but few know Sign. Those who are Deaf find themselves in a peculiar position. All their lives they'd been told to use their voices, to be like everyone else, and yet in that halfway house between life and death, their silences are revered.

Yet with the passage of time and increasing rents, one Deaf club after another has shuttered. Remnants of Deaf clubs past have become crowded with these spirits aching to feel the full throttle of Sign coursing through their psychic veins once again. With a gush of breath, they enter the lungs of language itself but only for a moment.

The silence of ghosts is louder than sound.

Angela Morelli sat in her car facing the rear entrance to the Deaf club, but she did not step outside into the bright morning. She was afraid of what today would bring. Still, she had taken pains to look good. She had her bangs cut and her nails manicured, and she wore a simple navy blue top and jeans. She was proud of the fact that even in her fifties, she looked damn good. But being the president of the board of trustees in charge of the Deaf club these days was extremely difficult, especially when its finances were in questionable shape. She looked up at the nondescript building.

A hundred years ago the brown brick building sitting on the corner of Oak and Bryant Avenues was always filled with Deaf people. They came there to socialize, watch subtitled spoken English movies, and take part in fundraiser dinners. The building was filled with plenty of light from the windows. The upper half of these windows had beautiful stained glass, which cast a soft-colored glow on everyone's signing. The hardwood surfaces on the first and second floors always shone, as if polished by spirits sweeping with their feet. When closed-captioned videotapes, and later DVDs, became prevalent, the number of people who showed up every night began to shrink. Then came the ubiquitous pagers with the built-in ability to send and receive emails and instant messages, and the free videophones from voice relay services. Suddenly expensive TTYs were consigned to closets. People no longer felt the need to gather and see each other face to face, and each new batch of young interpreting students would appear at the club, only to be disappointed by the few Deaf regulars. A few decades earlier Deaf people would've been suspicious of these novice signers, but the few who were still around did not pay these eager-faced signers much attention. The folkloric stories that Deaf people used to pass on down from one generation to the next became harder to find. Then young deaf people, usually outfitted with cochlear implants more often than not, were frustrated by the silences that now filled the club. Where were their own kind? Later, the club opened a small bar with a huge high-definition television screen that showed one captioned sports game after another at near-maximum volume in the basement, where volunteers sold burgers, hot dogs, and fries, but it wasn't enough to compete with the ease of social media and flashy hearing bars. After all, the Deaf club didn't have a liquor license. In addition to being a hundred thousands of dollars in debt, the club didn't have enough money coming in to help offset the bills and property taxes.

Upstairs on the second floor, where there was a

huge room that accommodated the overflow from the first floor and at times was turned into an auditorium for small theater productions, five people sat at a round table on a late Saturday afternoon. The club's board of trustees had been tasked with the question of selling the building to a hearing developer who wanted to divide the building into condos. The number quoted would erase the club's massive debt, but even if they did sell the building and paid all that was owed, they felt the aura of dread. If the local Deaf community did not have a place of their own, where would they go?

As the president, Angela had been thinking about all of this since their previous meeting when she broached the subject of selling the building. That was not a good meeting. Everyone became too emotional. She checked the time on her phone, took a deep breath, stepped out of her car, and walked into the Deaf club. Today she would put her own feelings aside.

Having already seated around a round table upstairs, the others were waiting for her.

Small talk was out of the question.

She nodded. "Hello everyone. Seems should time go-ahead start. Now discuss-discuss figure-out do-do finish. Paper-work here. Copies distribute-all. Read f-i-n-e print finish?"

"Not-yet," Rick Walters said. "Busy-busy all-week." A retiree after working forty-three years at the post office, he had been the Deaf club's caretaker for the last seven years. He took great pride in his job, which entailed keeping track of the bar's till, mopping the floors, paying the utility bills, and washing the

　　　　　　　　　　　RAYMOND LUCZAK

windows twice a year. He liked to wear a railroad engineer cap and Carhartt overalls; it was his uniform. When he wasn't busy keeping the place in order, he played cards with his buddies in the basement and debated which football teams had the best chances of getting into that year's Super Bowl. He had grown up in a Deaf family.

"Me-same," Paul Xerxes Yarsden said. "Sorry." Known by his name sign created by fingerspelling "X" downward in a "Z" movement into the letter "Y," the club's treasurer was in his early thirties. He worked out four times a week, so he often wore muscle shirts. Even though he was technically hard of hearing and could speak very well to be understood by almost anyone, he considered himself Deaf and preferred not to use his voice outside of his job at a hearing company.

"Read finish." As a member of the Springs, a prominent Deaf family, Michelle Spring-Sands had grown up in the community, so she was naturally too familiar with its internal politics. Now in her late twenties, she was a Gallaudet graduate with a perfect 4.0 GPA, but it had been extremely difficult to find a teaching job. Too many students had been outfitted with CIs, and hearing parents did not want Deaf people to teach their kids. They wanted only hearing teachers.

Everyone turned to Shawn Pickett, a bald attorney in his forties, and the club's secretary. Prior to the bout of spinal meningitis that took away most of his hearing while young, he had been used to having headaches and the occasional bout of tinnitus, but once he became deaf, the headaches and the tinnitus evaporated. He was afraid that if he got implanted, the headaches would return. Hearing aids were sufficient for his job. "Contract show-to two different lawyers, look good. Contract point-key-clauses expound-in-detail can."

Rick waved for everyone's attention. "Contract good? If only-you decide a-l-l, sign-contract would?"

Everyone looked at each other and started to remember things about this place.

ANGELA MORELLI, PRESIDENT
(1963-)

Angela stared at Rick. She wasn't seeing him at all; only seeing beyond him into the thin veil of time: the smell of flour being brushed off the kitchen counter after Grandma had finished rolling the fresh dough through the pasta cutting machine. The waft of tomatoes, olives, and herbs stewing in the stockpot. The distinctive nose-itch from the pot roast beef still cooking in the oven. The boisterous laughter of her father and uncles as they tumbled into the living room and everywhere else in Grandma's big house. The weary smiles of her aunts as they carried in big casseroles of cooked vegetables, all covered with foil. The antics of her cousins as they chased each other up and down the stairs to the foyer of the house. They had gone to Mass the hour before, so everyone was naturally hungry. Angela had sat in church, trying to lipread the stone-faced priest and trying to look interested in him as she daydreamed. She was always happy when Mass was over.

When she ate at Grandma's house, she always sat next to her older sister Marie. She loved the food, but she still felt a hunger to understand what could be so funny from the way everyone had carried on and laughed. They ricocheted off each other with wisecracks and an occasional admonishment from Grandma. When the sisters were younger, Marie did not seem to mind repeating to Angela some of the things said around the table, but now that Marie had become a sullen teenager, she wasn't in the mood to help anymore. When Marie left home for college, Angela felt truly stranded. At fourteen, she contemplated escaping these Sunday gatherings altogether, but she knew she'd never hear the end of her mother's conniptions. The older Angela became, the more resentful she became of these Sunday gatherings. Even her younger cousins were already joining in with their remarks, which the adults usually reacted with acerbic comments and chuckles.

School was even worse. She sat in the front row and lipread all day long. She couldn't always follow the discussions, but as long as she did her homework, she did all right. Then a hearing classmate asked her if she'd seen the piece about Gallaudet College on *60 Minutes* the night before. She was stunned. A college for Deaf people only? And they used … sign language?

She had been banned from using signs for as long as she could remember, so she went upstairs to the guidance counselor's office and asked Mr. Schmitt if he had information about Gallaudet. He didn't, but he said he would get the information for her. Later, when she applied, she was surprised to learn that Mr. Schmitt had never told her parents about her interest in Gallaudet. Everyone assumed that she would follow in her sister's footsteps and go to the university an hour's north of the city, but she never applied there. She wanted only Gallaudet, and she cried when she opened the letter of acceptance. She hadn't thought she'd be good enough to get in. That was when Mom found out, and as a result, her entire family was in an uproar for a few weeks. They couldn't believe that she was going over a thousand miles away to a college they'd never heard of, and in a city five times the size of the city they lived in. Much to her relief, Dad agreed to help pay for her college expenses, but only for the first year. He made it clear that if she could come back home and finish out the rest of her college years at her sister's alma mater, he'd pay for everything. The prospect of not having money for the last three years of college intimidated her, but she knew she had to go. Just *had to* go.

Her plane ride there was frightening. After pulling along her suitcase from the baggage claims area, she saw a lithe young blond woman in a T-shirt and shorts holding up the handmade sign MORELLI. Her stomach lurched. What had she gotten herself into? The stranger introduced herself, mouthing and signing slowly: "Hello, my name is Mary." Angela found it a bit disconcerting at first to have someone communicate with her without using her voice. Nevertheless, she got into Mary's car.

Entering Washington, D.C., was disorienting with

its traffic, but she wasn't prepared for what followed after Mary brought her into the sunny Ely Center. There, she got a huge shock. No one was using their voices! They were signing. They were smiling and laughing and ... She didn't understand Sign, but that didn't matter. She didn't have to rely on her hearing aids or wear her eyes out from lipreading; hands were much easier to follow than the tiny movements of tongue and teeth partially hidden by lips. She couldn't get enough of Sign. She was no longer lonely. She was indeed home among these strangers. She somehow knew she would learn their names in due time.

When she returned to her family for the winter break, her family fell into upheaval when they saw how she wasn't going to sit there and be quiet like before. She became vocal about wanting to know what was going on. When Uncle Tony said, "Oh, come off it—it's not really important," she exploded. "So I'm supposed to sit there and pretend I understand everything? No."

Everyone was stunned.

Then Aunt Molly began telling another one of her tall tales.

Before they knew it, everyone was chuckling as if Angela's outburst had never happened.

She leaned toward Mom, who happened to be sitting next to her, and asked, "What did Aunt Molly say?"

"Shh. I'll tell you later."

"No." The volume level of her voice surprised even her. "Tell me now."

Everyone stopped and looked at her.

"I'm tired of not knowing what's going on. I'm tired of feeling left out. I'm amazed that nobody's noticed that I don't laugh. It's because I can't follow what's going on."

"Oh, I thought you were just a moody girl is all," Uncle Phil said.

"You just don't care whether I understand anything. I'm just good enough for family pictures." She left the table, grabbed her jacket, and went out for a long walk along snowy streets. *Never again,* she kept thinking. *I'm never coming back after this break.*

When she returned home six hours later, the house was silent. She went upstairs to her bedroom and cried herself to sleep. The next morning Dad took her aside and said, "What you did was a real disgrace. Don't you ever show disrespect again, or I'll ..."

"Fine. I'm not coming back after this. Ever!"

"Hey. Don't get all upset now. Just don't do that again, okay?"

She spent the rest of her break silently packing the most precious of her possessions and shipping them to D.C. without telling anyone. She never saw her family again until she was in her thirties. By then she couldn't imagine being away from other Deaf people. Yes, she saw now that they could be as annoying as her own family, but at least she could understand *what* they were saying. She didn't have to work so hard on her comprehension, and she could laugh just as quickly with the rest of them. Now that Mom was dying of breast cancer, she felt obligated to return home.

Mom stared bitterly at her and said, "Thank you. All you've done was to make us feel awful about ourselves. Thank you." When she finally died, Angela chose not to attend the wake. Instead she found the Deaf club and sat with a group of people, some of whom she had met only once or twice before. She told them about Mom's death—well, pretty much everything else about her hearing family. She didn't care if she cried or laughed in front of these near-strangers. By the time she left the club, she felt incredibly relieved. Over the years as a job placement specialist, she had often given the new Deaf person in town directions to the club. But now? She had no ready-made answer.

MABEL HUBBARD BELL
(1857-1922)

For almost a hundred years I've been a ghost.

At first it was jarring when, after feeling the endlessly acute pains in my pancreas while not being able to see for almost a year, I saw the flickering aura of my spirit splinter from my broken body, still grieving for Alec, but there he was, his eyes misting tears of joy when I saw him at the end of the warm and strange tunnel. The tunnel had neither walls and a ceiling, and yet its shape felt like an ear canal leading close to the brilliant eardrum portrait of my Alec. I'd forgotten how his beard could seem aflame with its bright whiteness and his eyes could pierce me just so. I didn't need glasses anymore to see. In that moment of release I floundered because the pains in my last year didn't anchor me anymore. I hadn't quite understood that the body I'd inhabited for sixty-six years was no longer mine. I'd seen the dead bodies of my parents and relatives, but I'd never imagined myself turning into a corpse in my own bed.

I glanced behind me and saw that my daughters were

bustling around me, trying to revive me. I shouted their names, but they didn't react.

That's when I understood I was dead.

I looked down and saw that I had no recognizable form of body. I wondered what I looked like, but there was no mirror nearby. I could see only my hands. They gleamed like gold.

The feeling of warmth extended again from Alec. As I drew closer to him, I felt as if my head was about to explode from such pain. It wasn't the kind of swelling that accompanied a headache, but this was something else.

Then I heard his voice.

"Mabel, there you are!"

I was confused. Astonished, even. How was it possible that I could hear something so clearly? I'd lost my hearing when I wasn't even five years old. And I didn't have a problem stumbling like I always did when I walked in the dark. Was it possible that my innermost secret desire had been granted?

Floating about felt like such a miracle I thought I had gone mad. I was fully normal as I'd always wanted to be.

I didn't understand what I was hearing. I knew that Alec was speaking to me, but I'd never heard the full timbre of his voice before. He had been my speech teacher. That was how we'd met. I loved the way he looked at me. Sometimes his eyes made me feel hot as an iron poke left too long in the fire.

Then he invented the telephone. When other inventors accused him of stealing their ideas, I told him to get out there and fight for the goodness of his name.

We were lucky that Antonio Meucci died in 1896.

In those days, if the accuser died, the case died too. His children couldn't continue his case, so in the end, we won. Even Alec, embittered by the barrage of lawsuits against him, insisted that Congress recognize him as the official inventor of the telephone, which they did.

But what Congress did on June 11, 2002, was utterly disgraceful. They revoked their original recognition of my husband. The infamy!

No, you Deaf people stop lying about him. Alec did invent the telephone, fair and square!

No, you shush that talk about that trashy book The Telephone Gambit. *It's a crock of groundless speculations.*

No, you listen to me. All of you! I'm Alexander Graham Bell's wife, and that still counts for something. I'm not a historical footnote.

He married me, a deaf girl, at a time when normal men weren't interested in having deaf wives. He didn't have to marry me, but he chose to.

That's why my heart is a flame for him.

Still to this day.

I don't see him as often as I used to, but I know he still loves me. He is a genius, and he does better in the company of other geniuses.

My entire spirit wept with joy when I saw him waiting for me to slide out of my old life's ear canal into his.

He kissed me in front of everyone.

I thought I was going to die!

We'd rarely showed each other affection in public. We weren't that kind of people! Everyone was always watching us because we were the illustrious Bells, and we had to stay respectful no matter what new horrific lawsuit Alec was tangled up in. I was the lighthouse in each of his stormy days. Our girls helped light the way. He was so happy that each one of them turned out to be hearing. He insisted that I keep them away from Deaf people at all times. He didn't want them to learn the Deaf language. He wanted to keep them pure and normal.

He knows why I go to these Deaf clubs.

Because he can't. The combined rage of these Deaf people would surely kill him if he appeared in their midst. Just like how the Jews and others who'd died in the concentration camps had exterminated Hitler's spirit. Many awful men, when they die, often go looking for Hitler, and they're inevitably disappointed to learn that he couldn't hold on to his immortal self.

But I'm not hated; just disliked. It took me a long time to get accustomed to this hangnail fact of my life, but many of us ghosts are still young in the larger scheme of the universe. I've heard of ghosts who are thousands of years old, but many of them prefer solitude. They've tired of being grilled the same old questions about Jesus and Buddha and Muhammad. Nobody remembers their answers anymore.

My days are pretty much the same. In the mornings I visit with my best friend and check in with my daughters. I used to go to the grand infant daycare center and look upon the faces of my two sons, who'd died too young in my arms, but I stopped going.

A mother never stops grieving for her loved ones.

When I was a human, I never thought grief could be said to possess a discernible weight.

RAYMOND LUCZAK

Now I know differently. The weight of grief is heavier than any stone quarried.

Thinking of my two sons, I discovered that I could not move. I was bound as if to the earth itself.

After having been able to float quickly and easily across thousands of miles in a heart's beat, I felt as if my entire being had been uprooted and forced back into the same spot of quicksand. No matter how much I wanted to cry, I could not produce tears that could flood my hole enough to free me.

I had to stop thinking of my two babies. Too painful.

The nursery has over a million ghost nurses who tender each baby as if their own. That place is filled with love. Mothers who've never lost their children pitch in and help, but those who've lost their babies while human are still filled with anguish. Sometimes they have to be threatened with extermination, and they finally go away. No mother wants to die.

Alec said that he has never visited our two sons after he died. He didn't want to be heartbroken again.

He also said he's stopped signing upon his death. He won't even talk with his friend Albert Ballin. I wondered out loud if Mr. Ballin's book The Deaf-Mute Howls had upset him. It had come out eight years after Alec died.

"I said, 'No comment,'" he said.

I'm still proud of Alec. He is really a most brilliant man. He has better things to worry about.

I had seen the angry letters and protests that Alec had received from Deaf people who didn't want to speak. I admired his steadfastness. He knew he was right. The world was destined to be normal, and therefore Deaf people had to bend to the world, not the other way around.

No one wants me around when I visit a Deaf club, but visit I do. It's my duty to defend my husband's good name wherever I go.

It's never easy going into these places. I don't like the way their faces and hands move when they use sign language. They sometimes act like animals.

But you know what I feel for them? Pity.

They're carrying on and laughing. Just like normal people.

I can sense their eyes following me when I enter.

They say with their faces, There she is again.

They give me tight smiles but they never say a word to me. As ghosts, they may have bodies of shadow but their hands move like flickers of flame as their faces light up in Sign. Now that they could hear as well as I can, why haven't they chosen to speak? What's wrong with these people?

And what about my best friend Helen Keller? Of course, she can now see and hear. She did learn to speak, and she does very well, I should add. She has lots of friends. Just like I do. We are like sisters. We see each other every day. When I first met her, she was a little girl. I confess to having felt uncomfortable with her fingers touching my hand, and watching her demand that I fingerspell something in her hand.

Alec took her aside gently and fingerspelled something in her hand.

She then smiled and fingerspelled something.

Alec said, "She said it's a privilege to meet you."

I nodded.

Alec fingerspelled something in her hand. It seemed to take him a while.

RAYMOND LUCZAK

She laughed.

I asked, "What did she say?"

He said, "I told her that you're too smart to learn the deaf-mute language."

That was one of the many things I loved about Alec. He never said that I couldn't learn anything. He said I was smart.

I read a lot of books because I just couldn't lipread all day long. Reading words on a page enabled my eyes to rest because I didn't have to play the guessing game. Sometimes I found myself preferring to read interminably long books because they made for a good break from company.

I can still hear, but there have been times when I feel something has gone missing.

Do I want to lose my hearing again? Of course not.

Sometimes I think I visit Deaf clubs because I remember how Alec succeeded in changing the world for the better. He didn't want Deaf people to suffer the way his mother had. He was there in that eureka moment when Dr. William House, the cochlear implant inventor, realized what else he could try. Alec tried to use all of his energy to whisper, "Keep going," into that doctor's ear. Sometimes he got worn out by the shouting, and I wouldn't see him for days at a time. He was doing important work. Sometimes the best thing a scientist can do for another is to encourage him to keep going.

I'm the same way except that I'm a missionary.

I don't know why oralism has to be a bad thing.

I see so many Deaf ghosts, when given the choice to hear and speak again, refusing speech lessons. They've learned to do without speech, so therefore they see no need for speech. They love to sign, and sign they do. It's as if each room of every Deaf club, even if shuttered, haven't changed even though the humans have remodeled these rooms into offices and condominiums. When there are enough ghosts in the same room, what they remember collectively of the room from the time when they were alive reemerges as if the original details have never been altered.

This is another reason why I go. It's always astonishing to see these rooms return to their former glory, and so consistently. These places feel burnished as if with gold.

But when someone there gives me a cold eye, I suddenly remember why I've come.

I remind myself that these Deaf people are deluding themselves. They want to live in a more innocent time when being deaf meant signing all the time.

Oh, no, no, no!

Normal ghosts don't even bother to learn sign language. You'd think that normal ghosts, given their immortality, would want the opportunity to learn the Deaf language, but they never stop by these places. They know Deaf clubs exist, but they never go. They're too busy talking with each other, carrying on deep into the night and long into the day.

We ghosts don't like to sleep. We are like bees that way. Once a bee is born, she never goes to sleep until she dies. Even then ghost bees linger nearby, huddling in a protective orb surrounding their beloved skeps. They've never forgotten their great queen, and when her spirit rises and joins them, they go a-flutter with a mist of honey, emanating from their queen.

Sometimes I spend hours watching the humming bees.

I understand them in ways I can't explain. It's all about the work, and nothing else. They don't need to communicate anything else. Their world is simple. Their language is pure pheromone.

If only I could feel accepted by everyone in these Deaf clubs.

I travel from one Deaf club to another, because I expect that one day they'll realize I am a steadfast member of their community, and they must accept me as I am. They must understand that with their restored hearing, they've been given an extraordinary opportunity to speak. But they don't. They want to stay put where they are so when another Deaf person dies, they will be there to welcome their new member.

Watching them do this over and over again irritates me. Why not me? I've been around for almost a century!

This is where religion has helped me. The history of successful religions is rooted in dogged determination. All the great missionaries never give up. They were not accepted at first, but with patience, they were able to convert each lost soul after another.

As a missionary, I must never give up.

RICHARD ALAN WALTERS, CARETAKER
(1948-)

Rick stared at the small stage at one end of the big room and felt that familiar fondness surge in him. Many famous Deaf storytellers and poets had stood on that stage. He couldn't remember a time when the building wasn't in his life. Ever since he was a little boy, he was accustomed to chasing other kids his age around the club while his Deaf parents talked with their friends. His favorite game was Hide-and-Seek. He'd come to know all the best secret places that a child could hide, so it was a fun game to play with the new kids. Most people didn't know of a small tunnel that was designed as storage space right behind the backstage wall, and the door looked shut when it wasn't. He always won Hide-and-Seek that way. Sometimes he and his parents stayed there all evening, and it was something of a joke when they found Ricky sleeping on a pile of coats pulled off hangers. In fact, his first name sign was a one-handed version of the sign for "tired."

He thought for a long time that all Deaf people had parents who signed until the day his parents dropped him off at the state residential school for the Deaf. He saw tears in their eyes, but he wasn't too worried because his parents had gone to residential schools before. They explained why it was important for him to go to school. He thought it was strange that they'd say, "Every-one signs," as if it was an apology. Yes, he had seen hearing people everywhere move their lips to talk, but he thought that was a bit odd. Why did they use their lips when signing was more natural? That didn't make sense, but whatever. As he climbed up the monkey bars on the playground, he saw how other Deaf parents signed with his parents. Of course. They had to talk.

Then he noticed two adults with a young girl who wore hearing aids. Her parents looked about, unsure where to go; the girl looked about, confused. He was relieved when his parents simply pointed them toward the path to the main building. More and more children joined him on the playground. A few of them did not sign. He'd always thought that was odd. Why couldn't they sign if they were Deaf? His father had once explained that some deaf children were forced to wear hearing aids because they were supposed to hear people move their shark-like teeth while they chomp-talked. The expressions on his father's face always made him laugh. After his parents said good-bye, he felt a little strange but he resumed playing. He wouldn't quite understand until later what his parents had tried to explain to him why he was here at this school.

While climbing up the bars, he saw that girl again. Her parents bent down and looked her squarely in the face. They spoke something, and they looked like they were crying, but she didn't seem to understand. He thought it was strange that parents would use their voices to talk to a Deaf child. A woman, whom he later knew as Housemother Matilda, spoke and signed gently at the same time: "Please try not to worry. Your daughter will be fine." The girl's father wrapped his arm around her sobbing mother as they walked toward the parking lot.

Housemother Matilda brought the girl to the playground.

He got off the bars and ran to her. "Come-on, come-on," he signed.

She looked curiously at him. It was clear that she'd never seen signing up close before.

"Come-on, climb-bars." He was off and running. When he was halfway up the bars, he glanced back. She was running toward the bars. That was how he'd met Rachel Owens, the girl who later became his wife. He never got tired of telling that story. He liked her more and more as the years went by, but he never thought of her in that way, not in the way that boys spiked with testosterone would suddenly look at girls differently, at least not until he went out with Becky Spring and realized he didn't really want her after all. The next morning he went over to Rachel and asked her out. She was quite surprised, but she accepted. When he kissed her at the end of their first date, he knew he wouldn't marry anyone else. By that point he had known he was a simple man compared to his college-prep classmates. His grades were decent, but he wasn't interested in going to Gallaudet College. Soon after graduating from high school he found a job in the sorting room at the post office. He liked the work more when other Deaf employees joined him. Their easy company made their lunch breaks go faster.

When he took Rachel to meet his parents, they were so happy to meet her. Their first question had been: "Sign can-she? Yes?" Then it was no problem at all. Rachel liked them too, and she told them how disappointed she was in her parents for not learning Sign. Then Rachel found out that she was accidentally pregnant, and they had to get married sooner than later. That was how they ended up having their wedding at the club. The idea of getting married there started as a joke, but when they realized how cheaply the place could be rented, it was a no-brainer. The novelty of a wedding at the club drew more than the usual regulars. He never forgot the horrified looks on his hearing in-laws' faces when they saw how people signed and heard the occasional raw voice. In those days there weren't such things as professional interpreters, but he found a hearing signer who could voice for her parents and the few hearing relatives of hers. They'd thought that Deaf people would be silent in Sign, but that was not the case. They were easily distracted by the raw voices and the guttural laughs. It was a great day. Rick and Rachel didn't have the money for a reception, so they were very touched when a number of friends pitched in to help pay for the food and drinks on the first floor, and a few guys roasted brats and burgers outside. The food wasn't fancy, to be sure, but most people weren't there for the food. They were there to mingle. The more he saw the hearing world, and particularly her family through his wife's eyes, the more he felt proud that he could count the Deaf as *his* people. The fact that they didn't seem as shocked as hearing people by the speed with which they'd gotten married endeared him to them.

Then they had four children, half of which were Deaf, and the other half hearing. He felt a bit of disgust when he saw how his in-laws oohed and ahhed over their hearing children, and one of his Deaf kids asked him, "Them-two sign not why?" But he was always secretly pleased when he took their kids to picnics outside the club. He wanted to make sure that his hearing kids would use Sign. He knew that because the world was hearing, these two kids would assume the mantle of speech anyway.

As their children grew up and moved away, Rachel went back to school and learned how to do data entry, so she earned extra money. They went on small vacations in other cities where they met up with their Deaf friends. They spent more and more time at the club. Empty nesters converged there to socialize. They often played cards. As they aged, it seemed as if they knew of one or two Deaf friends all over the country dying one by one each month. The number of people who showed up to visit eventually shrank from eight tables down to five. A few of his friends had moved

RAYMOND LUCZAK

south to Florida where the weather was kinder to their arthritis. Later a few more couldn't climb up the stairs; the building didn't have an elevator. Then Rachel broke her hip in a car accident. The recuperation and the hip replacement surgery took her months, and he stayed at the house to look after her. When she was strong enough to step up into the club, they were dismayed to find that the number of card tables had been reduced to only two. It was then he realized nothing was ever going to be the same again. Young people still showed up, but always at the wrong time, which gave them the unfortunate first impression of emptiness. He had seen many of them all over the city, so the numbers were indeed there. They just weren't interested in hanging out at the club.

When the legendary caretaker Arnie Lott died, the board of trustees asked Rick to take over. It was perfect timing. Two years of retirement had made him quite restless, so he was happy to be given that huge ring of keys.

And now this offer from a major developer. When the club was built, the neighborhood was respectably middle-class with many family houses. In the last decade, the neighborhood had become quite trendy with boutiques and coffeehouses surrounding the club, which was starting to look rather dull in comparison. The building had become prime real estate.

As much as he didn't want to let go of the club, he'd seen the finances. They didn't even have five thousand dollars in the bank! The annual property taxes were much more than that. They had tried fundraising events, but not enough people came. Everyone had expected someone else to take up the burden, but no one did.

OLOF HANSON
(1862-1933)

At eleven years old, I lost hearing in one of my ears in an ice-skating accident. It was unsettling to listen one-sidedly to everything around me, but I adapted. I lived on a farm north of Fjälkinge in Sweden.

The following year Pa suddenly took sick and died. Our family trip to Minnesota where he'd bought a farm sight unseen had to be postponed.

Two years later, after arriving in America, I began to notice that I was gradually losing the rest of my hearing. No one knew what was causing such loss. One morning I woke up and found unable to hear again. I thought for a moment that I had died just like Pa. If I couldn't hear a word, it must've meant I had become a ghost. But I hadn't.

I prayed again and again to God that He restore my hearing. But He never did. I went to work on the land. I shoveled out my rage. What else could I do?

I was no longer a hearing boy who wanted to master the strange-sounding English language. I could still speak Swedish, but I didn't know how in the future my speech would gradually decline into imperfectly formed words, laced with my sharp accent. I tried to mimic the English words I saw on the lips of strangers and friends of my family, but their reactions made me realize that I had to learn the language of hands.

Then it was time for me to attend the Minnesota Institute of the Deaf in Faribault. It was frustrating at first because I didn't want to believe that I was condemned to using Sign. I was still praying every night to hear again. But the warmth of new friends in my new language made it possible to believe that perhaps not all was lost. Charlie Thompson became my best friend. I could still learn, and my teachers encouraged me to draw the buildings I liked.

It was not long before I went to the National Deaf-Mute College in Washington, D.C., and found my calling. The college offered a master's degree in architectural studies, so I studied the language of blueprint and the punctuation of construction as well as I had mastered Sign. Indeed my hands, thus bestowed with the ability to convey distance and height, proved later to be an asset when I needed to communicate with hearing clients and foremen on location. My Sign elocution had to be precise for there was no other way to be. Designing each new building so that there is no room for misunderstanding and therefore no cost overruns is painstaking.

Now that I was the first college graduate in my family, I found a position with the office of Hodgson & Sons in Minneapolis, Minnesota. I decided I needed to expand my visual vocabulary so in 1889, I traveled for ten months around Europe. Then I was asked to design the new Pennsylvania School for the Deaf.

A year later I returned to Minnesota, and being without a job, I had no choice but to become a teacher. Many Deaf schools around the country were hungry for Deaf instructors. A lack of teaching experience was not a hindrance to hiring; a college degree was all I needed.

I liked my students very much, but I was a miserable teacher. I wanted to design and build, not teach. My entire being wanted to be the force behind each new building that sprung up around the small town of Faribault.

I fell into the habit of inspecting the progress of each new construction. I sometimes drew design elements that I liked on my pad.

Then I met a lovely teacher named Agatha Tiegel. I'd heard much about her because she was the first female to graduate from my college. She had entered the college a year after I graduated so we didn't meet until she became a teacher in Minnesota. Mr. Gallaudet initially had qualms about admitting women to the school, but she proved that there was value in admitting female students. There had been much talk of her valedictory speech, which she entitled "The Intellect of Woman."

With her, I felt as if I could dream again.

I set up shop on Fourth Street in Faribault. My office looked out from the second floor. I toiled long hours in that office, but I was never happier. I had to work twice as hard to prove that I was as capable as other hearing architects. At least I had a few client referrals.

The good word about me soon spread. My buildings began to appear in far-flung places such as Alaska and Venezuela.

But it became harder and harder to seek new clients

when being an architect wasn't so unusual anymore. Many young hearing architects entered the field. They had priced me out of business.

Hapless and bitter, I knew I wasn't designed for retirement.

Desolate, I sought the wide-open skies at the family farm. I needed to see something of my home country. I still had the occasional dream of waking up hearing and speaking Swedish again. But each time I saw Agatha, I knew such dreams were rubbish. She really understood me. We'd been both late-deafened and struggled with our hearing families. We were semi-mutes.

Even though I felt that God had let me down when He took away my hearing, I still held faith in His infinite wisdom. I went to church every Sunday. Sometimes, when I traveled on business to other cities, I sought out the local deaf church. I needed the solace that came from seeing a service in Sign.

When my body began to fail me, I sought peace in my church. What did God want of me soon to approach old age? He'd given me Agatha and three beautiful daughters.

I felt Him fill my spirit. I looked around the pews of deaf people watching Reverend Strom. He was a fairly good signer, but he was hearing.

The answer seemed so obvious.

I would become a minister. I would build new homes of faith for deaf people. They would feel truly home with God. They wouldn't need to struggle with lipreading and feeling lost as they had growing up with hearing families at church. They were tired of having hearing people tell them how to live.

RAYMOND LUCZAK

I would be a whole new architect. I would build a new church so wide and open and full of light so their hearts could see as well as I that God was indeed on their side. I didn't need a blueprint anymore, for the Bible had all the instruction necessary for redemption.

I traveled all over the Pacific Northwest where I helped deaf Episcopalians. Agatha went with me. These days were wonderful. We had friends everywhere. Deaf people welcomed us into their homes, and we often stayed up late, talking about politics, religion, and mutual friends, all in Sign.

In my day hearing educators mocked us because we chose not to speak. We were barbarians, a step backward to Darwin's apes. Yet if these hearing educators had taken the time to learn Sign, they would've seen as I'd long known just how our hands were blessed with divine eloquence. Sign is far more complex than mere broken English on the hands. It is no wonder human linguists are still reeling from the discoveries in their research. Where would hearing people be if Alexander Graham Bell had succeeded in his misguided mission to eradicate Sign? Hearing people's understanding of what it means to communicate with each other would have been that much poorer. Deaf people are crucial to their survival.

Who knew that our hands could be infinitely powerful?

I am glad that God had seen it fit to take away all of my hearing when I was thirteen. He wanted me to become a better and more compassionate person.

I still miss those days when my young architect's body was on fire with visions. Drawing and recalculating the measurements to match what I saw rising in my mind's eye could be as tough as farm work. Precision, precision. No ink blots anywhere.

I'm proud of the houses and buildings I've designed. From time to time Agatha and I like to float on a round-robin trip and see how they are holding up against the tick-tock of time.

You could say that I'm on a never-ending pilgrimage where I come pay my respects to the men who've worked hard to exact my blueprinted visions.

Many agree that the house I'd designed for Jonathan Noyes, a superintendent of the Minnesota Institute of the Deaf, was the nicest of all in Faribault. It still is.

But I always save my favorite building for last: Thompson Hall. When my best friend Charlie suddenly died of a heart attack, his friends wrote me a letter asking if I'd be willing to come out of my retirement to design one more building in his honor. He and his wife Margaret were well-known for hosting get-togethers at their house, and now the deaf community in St. Paul had nowhere else to go. Having been long retired from the practice of drawing blueprints, I wasn't sure if I was up to the task, and I wrote so in reply. A lengthy correspondence ensued, but they soon won me over with their earnestness. I returned to St. Paul and went straight to work. I felt alive again, because this time I would preach through my blueprints. In my mind Thompson Hall would become a church of sorts. It would be a place of congregation.

The new building that soon rose at the corner of Fairview and Marshall Avenues doesn't look ostentatious or conspicuous. There isn't a sign out front that announces *its purpose. Thompson Hall has ample sunlight, softened from stained glass. The small stage is high enough to enable everyone to see the speaker onstage. The kitchen on the first floor is big enough to cook enough food for a banquet. After all, deaf people do really love their banquets. Hearing people don't recognize them enough in their own world, so the deaf community needs to do it for their own members. Agatha and I enjoy watching them give one speech after another even if they can become long-winded at times. Don't they know what an honor it is to be feted? Otherwise we will become forgotten quicker.*

Deaf clubs are the closest thing to a church my people can find anywhere. Granted, these places do not hold regular services designed for spiritual awareness and examine their own moral lives, but each time they get together is filled with small rituals. They hug. They spend time really talking with each other. They're nothing like hearing people who typically engage in small talk after service and hurry home. They linger. Just like ghosts do.

PAUL XERXES YARDSEN, TREASURER
(1986-)

Xerxes always felt that he had been born too late. He'd have liked to be born in the 1950s when the Deaf community was much stronger. In those days everyone got together at a club, and every event there was always packed. It seemed that every city had its own Deaf club, so it was easy to find temporary homes in the language of hands anywhere. He felt a kind of melancholy whenever he thought about how beautiful it was when two signers connected and felt as if they couldn't stop talking all night long. It was as if the more they signed, the more they would expel energy against the dark forces of oralism and audism. He also longed to have witnessed the 1960s, a time when Deaf people were beginning to be heard on their own terms, starting with William Stokoe's radical linguistic assertion that American Sign Language was indeed a bona fide language comparable to any spoken language and the controversial airing of *NBC Experiment in Television*'s episode showing in 1967 a number of Deaf actors conversing in ASL, rather than miming, unlike the Deaf actor Bernard Bragg on his show *The Quiet Man*.

Deaf since birth, he'd grown up oralist. He had sufficient residual hearing to enable him to lipread and speak quite well. His father was a Lutheran pastor in a small town, and his mother was heavily involved with the lives of their congregation. The youngest in his family, he had three older brothers who were very active in sports. He got along with them all right, but it seemed that whenever they joked around, he couldn't lipread them quickly enough to follow their banter. What could be so funny? Were they making fun of him? He could never tell. Then one by one, his brothers got married, moved out, and began having kids. Living alone with his parents unnerved him at first because the dinner table was quiet. There was no constant questioning of whether he was following the conversation. He could lipread and follow his parents with very little effort. This made him happy.

But one day, though, his youngest sister-in-law asked out loud during a rare lull in the conversation around the table: "How come Paul doesn't know sign language? Seems like it could help." She explained that a cousin of hers was an ASL interpreter, which she thought was really cool.

Xerxes was at first angry with her for talking about sign language. For one thing, Sign was completely unnecessary. He had gotten just fine without it. He had gotten good grades so far, so he didn't need the crutch of sign language. He was fully able to function on his own. But as he progressed through high school, the more he had to wonder if there was something more to the sign language thing. He kept his eyes peeled for anyone who wore hearing aids or cochlear implants, and he wondered if they ever signed.

But that wasn't as important as his big secret: he wanted to experience sex with a man. That all-encompassing fear of being found out was the reason why he worked so hard on his homework. He wanted to do well, so well that no one would suspect he could be "that way." He'd seen how some effeminate kids at school were bullied, and how the bigger kids would sneer with words that were very easy to catch: "faggot," "queer," "homo." He was grateful that he wasn't obvious like them, and that his older brothers had been well-respected athletes. If anything, he was a solid basketball player. He liked playing on the court. It was all about eye contact, so he did well.

A week after he turned eighteen and a month before he graduated from high school, he found himself completely unnerved in Martell's SuperMart where he was buying a bottle of ginger ale. A tall thin man in a T-shirt and jeans stood in line at the next checkout aisle. He too had a bottle of ginger ale. Xerxes was unused to a man looking him so intently. He wasn't sure what the look meant, but it suggested … he wasn't sure what it was, but he couldn't be … no. He couldn't be into guys, right? Of course, he'd known of gay people through the newspaper, but he didn't know anyone who was that way. When he paid for his ginger ale, he wasn't sure what to do. He walked slowly, wondering whether the stranger would follow him, debating whether to hurry on home. He glanced back and saw that the stranger was smiling openly at him. Xerxes decided to wait outside the store.

The stranger finally stepped out from the sliding doors. He signed, "You sign?"

Xerxes felt petrified. He didn't even know the manual alphabet! "I'm ... sorry ... but ... I ... don't ... know ... sign language." In retrospect, he felt truly embarrassed about how he'd first talked to Don Blake. He had talked just like a hearing person unsure how to talk with a Deaf person once he found out about his hearing aids.

"You deaf, right?" The stranger mouthed and pointed to him, and then to his own chin and ear before bringing down the fist of his index finger on top of the other.

He didn't know what to say. He'd never thought of himself as anything specific; just someone with a hearing problem. He never liked the term "hard of hearing." He looked up at the stranger. "I ... am ... I'm just ..." He pointed to his hearing aids.

The stranger signed slowly. "O-k."

They walked to a nearby park where there was a pond with ducks paddling about. There, on the bench, Xerxes began to learn Sign. The first sign he learned was "deaf." He hadn't anticipated it until then, but with each sign he learned from Don, he felt the ambiguities of his existence falling away, as if his shoulders were indeed feeling lighter. It wasn't until he stopped using his voice, stopped worrying about what hearing people thought, that he hadn't realized just how hard he had been working just to pretend that he had only a hearing problem.

That summer after graduation was glorious. He fell in love with Don, who'd suggested that he drop the boring first name Paul and adopt his middle name Xerxes for his new name sign. He also brought him to the Deaf club. He never forgot the first time he entered the building. It was an eerie feeling to sense how much history its walls had seen, and how much emotion its windows had seen. At first glance, it was a nicely maintained older building with some beautiful woodwork and polished hardwood floors, but knowing that it was home to the Deaf community gave it a patina that was impossible to remove. By then he had read up on the turbulent history of Deaf people. Don was a sophomore at the local university, so Xerxes learned how to request ASL interpreters for his classes. Didn't matter if he wasn't fully fluent in ASL; he needed to see ASL as much as possible. There was something powerful and compelling about hands moving to say something in ways that a mere voice couldn't. He knew that silence in the name of deafness was a cliché, but he did find the idea of silence, as opposed to having to make sounds with one's own voice, quite powerful. It soothed his very soul.

Xerxes was supposed to live with his parents while he attended the university, but when Don asked him to move in with him, he didn't hesitate. But he didn't know how to introduce Don to his parents. He didn't like to use his voice around Don because he didn't want his boyfriend to feel inferior, but at the same time he didn't want to turn off his parents. Worse yet, he'd never told his parents about learning Sign. He had simply spent less and less time eating dinner with his parents.

One night his father set down his fork and looked at Xerxes. "You've been out a lot. You seeing someone special?"

Xerxes stopped. "Uh."

"What's her name?"

He looked at Dad and Mom. "Uh. It's not a ... her."

Mom suddenly looked worried. "What are you saying?"

"I met a guy."

"What?"

"You heard me."

Dad stared at him. "Son, you sure about this?"

"Yes. And, uh, I want to move in with him."

The silence was thick as the aftermath of a flash summer rain.

"I don't know what to say," Mom finally said.

"You don't have to say anything. I'm just so happy with him."

"Paul?" Dad said. "What's his name?"

"Don."

"How did you meet him?"

"Well, I was at Martell's, and there he was. I don't know how to explain it. It just happened."

"Wow," Dad said.

Mom sighed. "I suppose we should meet him."

"Uh. There's another thing."

"What?" Dad narrowed his eyes.

"He's deaf like me."

"Oh, that's good then."

"Well, he can't speak very well, so he uses ASL to communicate."

"ASL?"

"Sorry. American Sign Language."

"You know signs?"

"Yes."

"You know what? Enough already," Dad said. "You've disappointed us. We didn't raise you to waste those years of speech therapy in favor of … what do you call it again? Oh, right. ASL."

"Dad."

"Just get your crap out of the house."

Xerxes went upstairs and began packing. He never introduced Don to his parents, which was just as well. His boyfriend had zero interest in meeting anyone who was audist and homophobic, so a few friends showed up with Don to help Xerxes with the move. He didn't say good-bye to his parents.

Living with Don went swimmingly well. Now known as "X-Z-Y," he majored in Business Administration. He wasn't sure what else to study; all he knew was that he didn't want to become a teacher. He didn't want to start up a business either, but he felt that his degree would help him find a corporate job. Fifteen years later he eventually became supervisor of the Insurance Claims Processing Department for a large dialysis firm.

RAYMOND LUCZAK

One afternoon he decided to pay his parents a surprise visit. The mainstream media had become more LGBT-friendly in its reportage, so it was time. He pressed the buzzer next to the front door of the porch and waited. He had shaven off his stubble, made himself look presentable with a button-down shirt and khakis, and inserted fresh batteries into his hearing aids. Over the years he had thought about his parents and brothers often, but he never friended any of them on Facebook. He could surmise from their profile pictures online that his nieces and nephews were growing up, and that his brothers were becoming portly, either from a lack of exercise, sedentary office jobs, or just age. He was grateful that he'd been health-conscious enough not to end up fat like them. The wait in front of his parents's house felt interminable. He debated leaving the front steps when he caught a flicker of motion from the inner door. His mother looked confused at him for a moment, then exclaimed, "Oh, it's you!" Wearing a print dress and a sweater, she looked much older with deep wrinkles and exaggerated jowls, but after having long maintained a gloss over his memories of her, seeing her that old shocked him. "Come in, come in!"

As he sat in the kitchen while she made him coffee, he felt strangely discombobulated. Everything familiar was in its place, but something was amiss. Dad was away with his brothers for the weekend as he wanted to help build a treehouse for his grandchildren. He sat quietly as she carried on and on. It was so unlike of her; she typically asked a lot of questions. Then he realized:

She is my mother, but she isn't Mom anymore. She's too afraid of the gay question, the ASL issue. When it was time for him to leave, she made him promise to visit when Dad was home.

"You still haven't asked about Don, my husband. I'm still gay, and I still sign. That's not going to change."

She sighed. "Why must you be so political?"

When he left the house to catch a bus crosstown to his apartment, it hit him what was so odd about the kitchen. It, and the house, was no longer his home. It was just a house he once knew a long time ago. He felt enormous pangs of sadness, but he knew he wasn't the only one who'd felt orphaned by their hearing families. He had to take comfort in that fact.

When the club's board of trustees asked him to become their treasurer, he automatically said yes. He would help preserve the club. One day all those kids with CIs would grow up and realize that a large part of themselves was missing and seek out others of their own kind and discover Sign. Until then he needed to help keep the Deaf club alive.

ELEANOR ZABEL WILLHITE
(1892-1991)

When I died, the first thing I did after greeting my dad was to let him pull me up by my hand to the skies. I hadn't finished crying my tears of joy in being reunited, but he didn't care. I hadn't flown a plane for half a century, so I missed being up in the skies where I was in control, and high above the rolling prairie fields outside of Sioux Falls. The glow of September coated the grasses with a shawl of gold spread far and wide as my eyes looked. Floating upward I was shocked to see the skies, which I'd always seen as empty and blue, covered up as if in bubble wrap. So many spirits from the beginning of time had longed to have the ability to fly as if angels, and once up, they never wanted to come back to earth. It was crowded with their ghostlights. Sometimes they were so bright with ache that at night they lit the lands below as if day. This made it easy for anyone to seek out their loved humans on land and watch them sleep long enough to slip through the backdoor of their dreams and wave a simple hello before slipping out again. The empty streets were never lonely at night. Each prairie wind whipped each other into a mad joy of frenzy that their passions seemed to build a cyclone spinning upward. Buffeted, I felt like a pilot again. How I'd missed the winds!

The first time I flew my Pard, I knew he was mine, all right. It was worth every penny that Dad had sent to pay for it, so I used his nickname in honor of his generosity. My Pard handled the winds and hummed happily underneath my feet. I couldn't hear, but the plane became one with me in the air. Aviation historians would note that my Pard was an Alexander Eagle Rock OX-5 biplane, but I never saw him that way. He was my lifeblood. I always inspected every familiar inch inside and outside. I stood on his wings and wiped each window clean. Because he was mine, he was the most beautiful plane I have ever seen. I feel good that my Pard is safe and sound in the Southern Museum of Flight. Let them marvel at the fact that I was the first Deaf woman to earn a pilot's license. I simply wanted to fly like Lucky Lindy.

When on the plane I learned not to worry too much about my hearing passengers. I let them babble whatever they wanted and smiled as if I could lipread them perfectly because in the end I was all they had up in the air. They peered out behind me and saw the great quiltwork of farmlands and town blocks underneath them. They were never the same once they staggered with jelly knees off my Pard. I knew that their dreams would be limned with the endless horizon in all directions, and a few of them would return and ask me for more information. They wanted that ladder to the heavens where dreams, sure as stars, would unfold like clouds parting to reveal a far more magnificent

universe than our forebears had ever imagined. They
wanted to be the next Lindbergh, the next Earhart.

Floating high in the air, I felt a tremor rather like
a surge of electricity crackle from beyond the western
horizon. I didn't know then how my new world would
work, but I soon recognized her. Amelia. My heroine.
When I was human, I had often dressed like A.E. I didn't
care that I looked like a man, but in those days, one felt
that flying a plane was a man's work so therefore men's
clothes were suitable. There she was: the spirit of her. I'd
long wondered as had so many others where she'd gone
in the Pacific. The answer didn't matter to me anymore
because she was right in front of me. Gazing at her face
I felt with a startle the former reality of being old: she,
freckled with a gap-toothed smile, was forever 39 years
old. I was almost a hundred years old when I died.

She mouthed, "Nellie, how have you been doing?"

Each time with her when human made me wish that I
had the ability to speak clearly, but that had never stopped
me from using my hands to gesture that I was well. At age
two, I'd lost my hearing due to measles, and I was sent
to the South Dakota School for the Deaf. I learned that
being Deaf was a badge of honor and pride. That I was
female was secondary. What mattered was that I had my
friends.

I was fortunate. My hearing father never made me
feel like I was any less than anyone because I couldn't hear.
I was not much of a student, but in those days you didn't
always need a college degree to secure a good-paying job.
I never felt like I had to worry about anything. I was to
graduate from high school and stick my wet finger up to

the wind, and see where it led me. The winds tumbled from anywhere off the plains, but they never told me where I should go. At first I stayed in Sioux Falls and took in the silents at the Orpheum. I liked looking up at the screen. Not knowing what they were truly saying to each other between the intertitles enabled me to dream all sorts of things.

I never wanted to be an actress like Granville Redmond, a Deaf man I'd heard who was good friends with Charlie Chaplin, but I knew I was a dreamer.

Oh, you know as well as I how easy dreaming is. You stop seeing things right there in front of you, and you start to see a movie screen except that you're not in the dark. You're not in the middle of a theater where cigarette smoke rises in a hurl of haze against the screen. You're in the thick of things. Everything unreal in front of you is in full color, and without any tint. Things happen in front of you, and you react in your own mind to these events and even people who have no business being there at that moment but inexplicably are.

No, dreaming's easier if you stop thinking of yourself in a movie. No more acting. You simply do.

The minute I read about Lindy making the first transatlantic flight across the ocean between Mineola, New York, and Paris, France, I felt as I'd been waiting the first thirty-five years of my life for something grandiose. I finally had a calling. I gazed up at the skies with fresh eyes and watched hawks hold their wings before making yet another swoop for mice skittering among the prairie grass for hours. I wrote a letter to my dad. I needed money for my flying lessons. Nobody talked about interpreters, but that never stopped me. I would have a pile of pads and pencils for classes. My father sent me a check for $200.

The few male students in my class looked askance at me. That they were hearing made me laugh inside. I knew how some men desired me, but I was a good girl. I never misled them; not ever. I think they willingly misled themselves when it came to answering my after-lesson questions.

I had to memorize a lot of formulas—the amount of fuel versus velocity, weight, and altitude. I aced all my written tests. That I was a woman no longer young and of marriageable age helped me navigate the occasional sneers of men younger than I who'd thought me incapable. My deafness was an advantage because I didn't have to hear the full brunt of their negative talk. I had no use for it.

With each hour spent behind the controls, I felt more and more complete. I was a wisp. I was a bird. I was sky itself.

My first time above clouds felt like falling in love. I had men interested in me, but they never elicited in me the same response I had from seeing the crisp blue-gray outlines from above, and the sun was above them in the distance. I felt powerful. I didn't know it was possible for a female to feel this mighty, but I did.

I was never afraid of flying even in stormy weather. I studied meteorology and the then-unreliable science of weather forecasts.

Eventually, with my pilot's license in hand, I needed a plane of my own. I lipread budding pilots talking about the planes they wanted to own, but I already knew what I wanted. That Eagle Rock biplane, parked perfectly in the hangar, was my siren. He kept flickering lights in my eyes.

I couldn't hear him but I could see him as mine.

My father wrote back to say how proud he was of me.

I told him that I would fly to Sheboygan and pick him up for a ride one day. Which we actually did a few years later.

Either way I had scored the money for my Pard. I went barnstorming. That was oodles of fun. I learned to do the loop-the-loop and swoop low like the hawk I was, and timed the moment when my sack of flour would drop out of my door. I hit my targets better than anyone. Those flour bombs weren't just a test of calculating velocity and height; hitting the red spot painted on the vast field as spectators watched was also an act of oneness with the wind.

The federal government soon stepped in and said that the days of barnstorming were over. Too dangerous.

Then I carried airmail. I was the only Deaf pilot who had ever done that job.

Eventually I had to sell my Pard. It was during the Great Depression, and I needed money. Then, of course, my dad died. Sometimes I visit my Pard in his museum.

Then came along the second world war. I ended up inspecting propellers before the warplanes went overseas. I wanted to fight, but they said that women and Deaf people weren't allowed to be soldiers. I was to stay put and help.

I taught waves of young people how to fly. But most of them weren't pull-up-by-the-bootstraps dreamers. It was becoming a respectable profession with none of that gritty glamor of yore. Each airline had its own uniform. Each new plane that rolled out each year was bigger and wider and heavier with a new coat of paint that shone.

The rest of my days felt like a tumbleweed from one

end of the plains to another, and back again. I looked at the skies every single day and wondered how it would be like to fly there in that moment.

When I boarded my first commercial flight, I felt neutered. I sat next to a window and saw the long concrete runway ahead of us. The plane was much bigger, and it had a great many more passengers than in my time. I looked back at them. The sense of awe and wonder that came from conquering the physics of gravity after mankind having pondered for centuries the question of how to fly didn't appear on their faces. I felt again the well-worn sadness that came from missing the hum of my pilot's seat and coasting miles high above the prairie.

Ever since my death, I have taken to floating as if in my Pard except that I have no wings. There is no seat nor an instrument panel. My spirit has my own compass. I go where I want to go, and there is no need for checking weather conditions before taking off. You can spot those who used to be pilots. They restlessly traverse from one end of the globe to another. They hunger to recapture the same sense of purpose they once had. They miss the human instinct to protect themselves from fatal danger.

I used to be one of them. These days I find myself wanting to nest like a bird. I find a tree and perch myself there to watch below the humans bustle about as if they're all alone in this vast universe of ours. Sometimes my dad joins me, but I don't think he understands why I pick these particular spots to haunt.

Back when I was flying, I never spent much time at the Deaf clubs. I was too busy barnstorming all summer long and on weekends too. I never got to see many of my Deaf *friends grow old and disappear; many of them left South Dakota for elsewhere. These days I hop from one Deaf club building to another. I like to watch people go in and out of them. Makes me feel good that they still have a home of their own.*

And then, when the weather of my loneliness gets too much on my perch, I swoop into the Deaf club and smack dab in their midst. All my ghost friends laugh when they see me coming. My former classmates and their spouses are like the siblings I never had growing up. They are my true family. No matter which Deaf club I'm in, each gathering is always a family reunion.

RAYMOND LUCZAK

MICHELLE SPRING-SANDS, VICE PRESIDENT (1990-)

Michelle never thought that her growing up as a member of a seventh-generation Deaf family would bestow upon her a covetous standing within the community. Classmates at Gallaudet were envious of her family background; she was "Deaf-strong" in ASL parlance. But very few people knew that Michelle had very mixed feelings about her heritage. In her state there were a few prominent Deaf families because of intermarriage. Michelle's parents had given birth to four boys and two girls, all Deaf; these four boys married other Deaf women, so that meant four more Spring wives. Some of these female Springs had come from other Deaf families, so family reunions often felt like a collection of tribes unified by a few common names as opposed to just one. These families always made a point of knowing which of their ancestors had married into other Deaf families, and tracing their lineage generations past. They also never forgot their ancestors' name signs while passing down family stories.

Michelle loved these stories, and she didn't mind it when Uncle Joe had to tell it again to a new child. Everyone knew the importance of sharing Sign with their children. Their hands would spread Sign like dandelion whiskers floating about on the wind, and Sign would take root in these tiny hands, seeing the light of understanding as easily as the sun. From there, these children would grow up socially confident unlike their non-signing deaf peers; they never experienced the hesitation that so often came with never feeling sure about one's own language. They were taught never to be ashamed of the fact that they couldn't always speak clearly or if they chose not to speak; being crystal-clear in one's signing was more important. Sloppy signing was inexcusable. Years later, when she entered the National Technical Institute of the Deaf in Rochester, New York, a few of her formerly-mainstreamed classmates remarked on the clarity of her signing. She was often asked to perform in stage productions at NTID, and many in the know could see that from the crisp dialect of her signing, she was a Spring. Had to be—native signers were always right with their guesses when meeting her for the first time.

By the time she graduated from NTID, she knew she didn't want to marry a Deaf man. She had seen the goings-on among her relatives, and while it wasn't technically incestuous, it did feel that way. For instance, a cousin from the Hawkens family was married to her uncle from the Spring family; the Springs and Hawkens could claim to have had two more distant blood connections in their background. She also tired of the arguments that flared up at the big gatherings, and she didn't like how everyone had seemed acclimated to these jealousy-fueled outbursts. Divorce complicated a very messy picture, so Michelle knew enough not to ask questions about how they were doing right after they saw their exes on the other side of the room, or she'd get an eyeful, which were sometimes graphic, right down to the ex's favorite sexual acts.

Unlike most Deaf people with hearing parents who'd never bothered to learn Sign, she longed to have had Sign-fluent hearing parents. She longed to attend a family reunion where none of her relatives were connected to other Deaf-strong families but to other people who had lost their hearing due to non-genetic causes, so she would have some privacy. She wanted to tell all of her relatives that they needed to grow up and let bygones be bygones, but she knew they'd never listen. The language of hands was so linked to the circulation of blood that it was impossible to stay neutral in the war zones of the heart. There was also the issue of dating a hearing man. She knew that her family and relatives would never forgive her if he couldn't sign clearly enough. If not a hearing man with no genetic disposition for deafness, she'd have to look for a Deaf man from a hearing family. That was her best option, really.

In college, she dated a few such men, but most of

them weren't fluent in Sign. They still retained an aura of oralism about them; they occasionally mouthed words in English while signing, or they put their ASL signs into the English word order. She knew how her family would comment: "Signing awful same claw-scratching-on-eyes." That was why she never brought a date home to meet her family; they'd grill him endlessly. Not good for a first impression.

When she landed her teaching job at a new Deaf charter school, she was happy to see that most of her students didn't come from her family or have indirect blood connections with her family. She was content with her quiet life, spending time with a few close Deaf friends a few evenings a week when she wasn't too tired from grading student homework. Then she had to fly to Washington, D.C., and attend Gallaudet University for a week-long conference. It was there she met Jeff Sands, a Deaf researcher who was reasonably fluent in Sign. The more she got to know him, the more she liked him. He had come from a hearing family so dysfunctional that he said if he had a choice, he'd choose a Deaf dysfunctional family because at least he'd know just what they were babbling about.

"True-biz? You-meet my family sometime."

"Deaf family?"

"Seven generations back."

"Wow."

She explained what her family reunions were like, and warned him that they wouldn't be kind toward him. At least not right away. He'd need to earn their approval before they welcomed him with open arms.

Months later, after many trips between her hometown and D.C., she brought him to meet her family at their annual July picnic. Of course, the Hawkens, the Gardiners, and the Vernes would be there; easily a hundred people. As she watched him try to maintain his composure while fending off some inappropriate questions, she felt a powerful overprotectiveness surge in her. She wanted to tell her family and relatives to back off. He was a studious guy who liked to observe; he did not like to jump to conclusions about anything until he'd learned all he could about the subject before making a decision. No wonder why she'd fallen so hard for him: he was drama-free.

That first night back in their hotel room he turned to her: "Me do-do okay? Honestly?"

"Wait tomorrow. Everything gain-gain worse will. Family that."

"Your family crazy same mine, but prefer your family. Honest, clear, easy-understand. Me not confused."

She wanted to marry him on the spot.

Then the research institute where he worked had another round of budget cuts. He lost his job and moved in with her. Their church wedding turned out to be insane. It felt as if two percent of the attendees were hearing non-signers who wouldn't dare walk too far from the poor interpreters. He thought the whole spectacle to be quite funny, because his hearing family was at a loss what to do with these people uninterested in using their voices for the sake of a conversation.

Then came their three children: two Deaf boys and one hearing girl. Her family was very disappointed that their third child was hearing, but Michelle and Jeff didn't care. They would just sign with her as if she was Deaf. With these children, she found herself drifting away from the club. Some of her stalwart relatives still showed up there to play cards. She just didn't have the time to socialize like before, and what's more, Jeff had been promoted with added responsibility at the local university.

When she was asked to join the club's board of trustees, her first reaction was: "Why me for-for?" Many of her Deaf friends didn't go to the club anymore; they preferred to socialize in each other's backyards where they could watch their kids. She used to know a lot of people who had gone to residential schools, but now it seemed that most of her friends had been mainstreamed and discovered Sign in their teens. Some of them didn't even learn it until after they graduated from college! Even if they wore hearing aids and cochlear implants, they were still good people. Their occasional awkwardness in Sign would've made them easy prey for her family. She kept them all away. But the more she thought about the opportunity to serve on the Deaf club's board, she sensed that if she pushed hard enough, they might find ways to attract Deaf novice signers, and make them feel welcome without feeling judged.

Eight months later she was utterly frustrated. The bickering between the volunteers and the board of trustees were much worse than she'd anticipated. The volunteers, though good-hearted, had their own ideas of how the club should be managed. Sometimes they changed the way they did things without warning the board of trustees, and that cost more money.

NAMELESS
(1957-1989)

You are a flash of face on the sidelines, eyeing the camaraderie of friends who've known each other for decades and now centuries. You have been Deaf all your life: still a stranger.

So many spirits are coming into the Deaf club that no one seems to know that you exist. Waiting to get called into the great mingle where just-released friends unexpectedly find each other and burst into tears of joy, you envy them. You've never had true friends even when you were human. Your life was all about doing just enough to get by. You've blended well into the background of grays. Your face, a dull glow, is etched in shadow.

You've tried a number of times to wave to someone you once knew in school or from work, but their eyes are already catching sight of someone else more beloved.

The border in front of you is made of invisible ice. You are not popular enough. You are not good-looking. You are just an ordinary Deaf person with no extraordinary talents. You are just another leaf on the branch. You long

RAYMOND LUCZAK

to fall off and get noticed. Perhaps someone will turn and ask who you are and where you've been all this time.

The border has an electrical fence that doesn't exist. You know it's only your imagination, but you are afraid of the shock of failure. Are you so unloved that you will never have a chance at being accepted as one of them? You breathe Sign, but you're not a scholar or anyone famous. You have worked in a variety of odd jobs all your human life. You knew a great many people, but they were all hearing. They had rarely tried to communicate beyond the basics.

It's easier to hide in the walls of shadow. The dimness makes it easy for you to hide your tears. Loneliness burns down your face. Loneliness is a permanent dagger in your spirit-heart. You ache to possess enough strength in your hands to pull it out. Sometimes you daydream ripping out that knife of bitterness and stabbing yourself over and over again. Maybe someone will notice you at last. You suspect not.

You make a lousy guest. You are just a signer who did nothing but watched TV. When you were human, you were too afraid to make a difference. You didn't want to be backstabbed. You didn't want to lose the few friends you had in those days. It was easier to do what you were told, and to work hard.

You cherish your hands, but they seem to have betrayed you. Over and over again.

When you first entered a Deaf program at a hearing school, you thought you'd find friends. For a time you did. Then you were considered an excellent candidate for mainstreaming. You didn't see your Deaf friends as often. You missed them.

You decided not to care anymore about your grades. You wanted to be with your Deaf friends all day long. You didn't want your classroom interpreter to be your best friend. Your parents were disappointed, but you didn't care.

"See?" you say to yourself. "Life story mine special not."

You may be just another lonely face in the crowd, but no one would know it. You've hidden your yearning to connect with another person very well. You act as if you don't need anyone for sustenance, but you are a vale of ache. Your soul is shadow.

You are nobody that nobody can name.

You long to break forth into Sign, but no one has sought you out for conversation. You watch familiar strangers exclaim at the end of yet another story being told.

You are no dazzling storyteller.

You were a hard worker who was forced to return to a small town when both of your parents took ill and needed someone to look after them.

You grew old quickly with each trip with them to the hospital, and back to their house.

Your parents didn't sign very well, so you three rarely had meaningful conversations.

Did they come looking for you when you died?

They looked happy for a moment, and then realized they didn't know your language.

You turned away. After all you'd done for them, the least they could've done was to interact with the spirits here and learn.

You learned about the financial woes facing the last

Deaf club in America. You flew there, hoping that someone would welcome you. Didn't matter if you were a total stranger. What should matter was that you knew Sign. Anyone could see that you weren't intimidated by their quicksilver signing. You understood all of them, but did they want to talk with you?

There are moments when you wish you could kill yourself. Decades of waiting can do that to your way of thinking. The problem is that you are already dead.

A deep part of you keeps hoping that someone will acknowledge you and beckon you to cross that border where your future family is. They would be the family you'd hoped to have once you realized your parents didn't love you enough to learn Sign.

But no one is waiting. No one!

You have no body except your face and hands, but your soul is dead tired. It is thirsty for a little affection. It needs the water of friendship. Just a glass would do.

You look again at the spectacle of reunions and reminiscences. Why aren't you with these people? You're Deaf too!

Or have you found yourself trapped in loneliness, the worst kind of purgatory?

You have no key to let yourself out. Who do you ask for that master key?

You have a startling thought. Are you truly alone?

Glancing behind yourself, you are startled to see an endless sea of faces with the same facial expression as yours. How could you have not noticed them? Who are these people?

You realize that you haven't been the only one haunted

with the desire to be part of the happy commotion in front of you. Lonely souls such as yours are many rows deep. You are among those Deaf people who hasn't sought attention or tried to fight for your community; everyone had their own reasons.

No. This isn't right.

You force yourself to cross into the edges of maelstrom. All these Deaf people are signing, but they don't seem to notice you at all.

Feeling dizzy after crossing such an imaginary border that's kept you chained to your spot for decades, you glance back again. Has anyone noticed you stepping away from the shadows? You tamp down on your feelings of giddy embarrassment.

You catch a skinny man's face watching from where you once stood. You beckon him to come join you for a conversation.

You hesitate. What if he thinks you're not for him?

The stranger glances around to reassure himself that you weren't talking to someone else. As he floats closer, the ice cube of your being melts. You feel warmth as the two of you trade names. The two of you dispense with small talk and discover that you'd spent your entire human lives seeking a home only to find it after death. Who knew that Heaven could be found right here on this earth?

After you and Joseph talk for what seems like days, you realize the problem. People used to come to Deaf clubs because they were lonely like you.

All you had to do was to look for another lonely soul as yourself and say hello. It is really that simple.

You spot another lonely face. A young woman with

tear-filled eyes. You wave your hand. "You search friend? Me-same."

Never have you seen a face turn so rapidly into joy.

Oh, how so easy to make another person happy!

You may remain a stranger to most everyone here, but what matters is that you now have a brand-new heart, throbbing and alive as if in flesh.

SHAWN STEPHEN PICKETT, SECRETARY (1975-)

When Shawn first got the letter from Allen Paulson, the CEO of the real estate developer Cookson International, he was quite surprised. A few months back he had met Allen at a fundraising party for a city councilor incumbent, but he didn't think much of the short man with round glasses. He was one of those hearing people who behaved as if he was the hottest thing since sliced bread, and pooey to those who didn't know it. Worse yet was how he'd rubbed Shawn the wrong way. He was sure that Paulson had meant well, but he didn't like being talked down to because he wore hearing aids. Or maybe it was because he was tall and imposing, and Mr. Paulson reacted to him the same way a tiny dog would toward creatures much bigger than him, behaving as if he had a bigger bark.

All his life Shawn had lived in limbo. He was hearing until a bout of meningitis took just enough of his hearing to make him hard of hearing at age five. Outfitted with the body aids, he required only minimal training in listening and maximum training in lipreading. It was different wearing the aids, but since he had already mastered speech and language, it wasn't too difficult a transition. He just had to remember to sit in the vantage point in a group conversation so he could lipread everyone. The gradual decline in his hearing wasn't that noticeable until he was thirteen. The audiologist told him that he needed more powerful hearing aids, and that his behind-the-ear models weren't strong enough. He'd have to go back to wearing body aids like a bra underneath his shirt. He hated it because each time he looked in the mirror, he saw an old man with youthful skin and clothes with the cords diving into his collar. He never saw another deaf person his age who wore body aids, and this bothered him a great deal. Yes, vanity was part of it, but it meant that he was far more deaf than he and his family wanted to admit.

Yet he was grateful that his hearing family made accommodations for him every step of the way. Everyone at mealtimes took turns talking; his parents liked this approach very much because it meant everyone could be heard without interruption. "Funny how having a deaf kid made us listen to everyone," his dad would always remark when he talked about his kids at the office. Even though his family was great, being a teenager was hard. He hated feeling like a dork, which affected his chances of asking Fiona Sampson out on a date. She had long black hair that was parted in the middle, she wore glossy red lipstick, the color of her eyes was ice blue, and her face didn't have a single pimple. If she had lived in New York, the Ford Agency would've snapped her up in a heartbeat. She knew she was quite pretty, so she never had a shortage of guys interested in her. In spite of her beauty, she was rumored never to have gone all the way with anyone.

Everyone in his senior class noted that Fiona had gone out with every boy in the class except for two. Derek Copper had a B.O. problem and came from the wrong side of town; he stuffed tobacco chew into his mouth and spat it outside during lunch breaks. After repeated visits to the principal's office, he was forced to keep his appearance to the barest levels of acceptability. Derek sat in the last row of every class, and he had barely passing grades. It was clear that he wouldn't go far in life. His father was a garbage collector who ran a junkyard on weekends, and his mother had left her husband and their four kids without explanation. No one ever bothered to keep their trailer home clean. It was rumored that the water out by the trailer park, which was a mile away from the tannery, was dangerous for consumption, and that was why the kids from those places were so ornery and disrespectful. Most of them dropped out of school because they got pregnant or had to find work to support their underaged girlfriends.

So: Fiona hadn't gone out with Derek or Shawn. He'd realized this long before everyone in his class figured it out; he'd kept hoping that she would finally show interest in him. She had broken up with Craig Whitehead, the least popular player on the football team. Even though he was a decent runner, he was usually benched during the important games. The boys who had gone out with her whispered among themselves and compared notes on why she broke up with each one of them. It seemed as if she was looking for the perfect boyfriend; the reasons didn't matter so much because it all came down to physical perfection. He felt that for sure, he would be the next guy to date her, but when two weeks passed, everyone wondered out loud if she'd suddenly gone gay. Didn't matter that she didn't have any female friends; none of the girls liked her. They were envious of the ease with which she went out on dates. So he waited. And waited. He began wondering if she'd met someone else outside of school and no one knew about it.

He watched her carefully in the hallways and in the classroom. There was something different about her. Then he noticed her touching her belly quite often. No. It couldn't be. Pregnant? No, that was impossible.

Two weeks later the news of her pregnancy broke. Derek Copper was the father. Everyone was mortified. Derek? Whatever did she see in him?! People began calling the couple Beauty and the Beast, but the beast was rarely in evidence. When he did show up, he had a permanent smile plastered on his scruffy face.

Shawn was filled with rage. How could she choose a low-down guy over him, who had so much to offer? Shawn came from a respectable family, and even though he was inexperienced, he knew he would make an excellent boyfriend. He had a part-time job as a filing clerk, working for his dad's best friend, who was one of the four attorneys in the small town where they all lived. He liked the job because it didn't involve telephone work. Sometimes he spent a few minutes reading the trial paperwork before he filed it away. Later, when he went to college, he decided to go into prelaw. He hadn't then known what else to do with his life. So at eighteen he had money saved up for college in his bank account. He could afford to take Fiona out on weekend dates at the A&W Drive-In, and if she wanted to see the latest Hollywood offering at the Porcaro Theater two towns over, he had money for that too. All she had to do was to express an interest in him. He felt a mixture of disgust and pity for her now that she was slated to marry Derek a few weeks before their graduation. She was supposed to go to the local community college, but he knew that wasn't going to happen, not with a baby on the way and a shifty slob like Derek.

The more he thought about the situation, the angrier he became. Did the bitch truly think that going out with a deaf man with serious college aspirations would be worse than going out with a sleazy guy with a major B.O. problem? What the hell was she thinking? He was quite sullen in those days, so much to the point that his parents asked him point-blank over dinner what was wrong. He told them about Fiona and Derek.

Mom said, "Oh, dear. You'll meet someone better. Just you wait and see."

Dad said, "Your mother's right. One day, when you come back with a nice-paying job, she'll be so sorry she didn't go out with you." He had been accepted into

Yale University with a full scholarship, which was a total surprise. He suspected that his dad's best friend had something to do with it, but he was never sure.

In spite of encouraging words from his parents, he didn't feel any better. He watched Fiona's belly swell bigger, which disappeared under her gown on graduation day. He felt a twitch of anger when he caught Derek kissing his new wife on the cheek after the ceremonies.

Yale proved to be an overwhelming experience. He had seen a little bit of the haves and the have-not mentality, but never to the jaw-dropping degree he saw among his wealthy classmates. Given his meager funds, he couldn't keep up with the Joneses on campus. Moreover he had to contend with the sheer amount of information that he had to absorb from long lectures in cavernous halls. He couldn't always hear the professor, or lipread him from the side as he drew on the blackboard. It was quite frustrating at times, but he forced himself to read each textbook closely. The language was often dry and boring, but eventually he learned to break down the bog of text into concepts that made sense. He came to realize that if he did the same thing with all his classes, he probably could pass without ever showing up in class. But he did show up anyway. He didn't want to be alone with his books all the time, and there were always pretty girls in each class. It wasn't like high school.

He got along quite well with his hearing roommate, also a scholarship student. He shared Shawn's fear of not maintaining his GPA required to stay on scholarship, so they both studied hard. Sometimes they went out to bars on Crown Street, but Shawn never went home with any of the pretty ladies there. The music was too loud, and the lights were too dim.

By the third year of college, he found his classes suddenly hard to follow. Granted, it was all pre-law, but fatigue was settling in. He couldn't figure out what could be wrong; he was just so *tired* all the time. He often felt like sleeping in and disappearing from the world, but his sense of duty and obligation kept him awake. He went to classes, but his eyes were already glazing over by the halfway point of each class. He didn't know what to do, so he went to the campus nurse. "I don't know what's wrong with me, but I'm *so* tired all the time."

The nurse interrogated him. "Are you taking prescription drugs? Recreational drugs?"

"No."

"What about drinking?"

"Beer once in a while, but I don't like bars."

"Okay." She glanced at his ears. "How well do you hear?"

"According to my audiogram, I'm profoundly deaf."

"You don't use sign language, right?"

"No."

"So you lipread all day long?"

He nodded. "Basically."

"Ah. One of my nieces is Deaf. She says that lipreading can cause some fatigue in some people. That's why she uses sign language interpreters. You should talk with the Disability Support Services in the next building over."

Having a notetaker in his classes helped, but it wasn't enough.

He was disappointed to learn that even though the university could provide interpreters on request, they didn't offer classes in Sign, but he learned where he could take classes in ASL off-campus. He wrote a letter to his parents and asked them if they could help chip in for the cost of his ASL class. He was so happy to get that check.

That first night in class he was nervous. Sitting among hearing people in a half-circle while waiting for their teacher to show up, he wasn't sure what to expect. All his life he had worn hearing aids, but he never needed to sign. He wasn't sure if this would be a good thing, but when he saw June Moorsky walk into the classroom at the James Hillhouse School, he suddenly felt at ease. She was clear with her hands and her facial expressions, and she was funny! He had never laughed so hard, and in a classroom? Completely unheard of. He began to wonder if being Deaf wasn't such a bad thing after all.

After three weeks of ASL, he knew he was madly in love. June was short, sassy, and smart. He was afraid that she was taken, but he didn't know enough Sign. He was so frustrated, and so afraid that if she was single, someone else would snap her up in a heartbeat. He couldn't wait until the next class night. He hadn't realized what a huge relief it was to turn off his voice for a change, and how relaxed his shoulders felt when everyone in the class signed instead of using their voices. Didn't matter that all of them were hearing. They were truly equal. But more than anything, he loved watching June interact with her students. He couldn't stop smiling when he discovered a new sign that he liked. He felt so goofy at times!

He didn't want the ASL class to end. His mind was abuzz with the finals that he had to study for, but when it came to June, his mind's eye was clear. He felt good about his fingerspelling, but he wasn't so sure about his signing. He waited for all the classmates to wander out of the room when he turned to June.

"Hello." He felt so awkward, but this was his last chance. He had to know.

"You o-k?"

"Yes." He felt a blush of crimson fill his face. "I … sorry." He had used his voice. "Me ask you o-u-t." Then he remembered one more crucial sign. "Question-mark."

She smiled. "Of-course."

He couldn't believe his luck. Just like that? He wanted to hug her and kiss her!

She wrote down where they could meet in two weeks. He would need to focus on his finals before interning at the New Haven County Courthouse.

They met again on a sunny evening. They sat outside a bistro, and he couldn't believe how much better it was to turn off his own voice. He was astonished that no one seemed to be paying attention to him or her. He was showing the world that he was indeed Deaf, and no one seemed to care that it was a big deal? Wow.

He learned that June was a graduate of the American School of the Deaf in Hartford, Connecticut. Before that, she had endured a speech program in which Sign was banned. Her parents, who were both doctors in two different hospitals, were enormously disappointed in her because she was an oralist failure. They tried every which way to cajole her into speaking, but she just didn't have the capability to speak clearly. Finally, at the age of twelve, she was transferred to ASD, where she blossomed after a few months of learning Sign from her peers. Shawn still thought it odd that anyone would forbid the use of Sign.

He was elated when she agreed to see him again.

She continued teaching ASL while he finished his prelaw studies. He didn't get accepted into the Yale Law School, which was just as well. They offered very few full scholarships for law students, and there was no other way he could afford the tuition. The student loan would've been massive. He got into the university law school an hour south of his hometown, and by then, he was a married man with a baby on the way. When their child turned out to be deaf, June was surprised by his parents' reactions. They were disappointed, but they asked a few moments later: "Where can we learn ASL?" She never got tired of telling Shawn how lucky he was with his parents.

When he passed his bar examination, he chose a large city near his hometown for a job at a medium-sized firm. By then he was now a father of three children. The other two weren't deaf, but June insisted that he not use his voice around them. She wanted all of them to master ASL first. The hearing world was all-English, so she wasn't worried about their mastery of English. They still went out to ASL-interpreted theater productions and participated in events at the Deaf club.

When their youngest boy was old enough to apply for college, Shawn got an unexpected email from Angela Morelli. The club's ASL-fluent hearing lawyer, who had been providing services pro bono for nearly forty years, wanted to sell his house and move south to Florida. Would Shawn be interested in taking over the position on the board? They needed a secretary, too. "Sure," he said, but he wasn't quite prepared for the politics simmering beneath the surface each time the board met. Even though he liked the board members, he too shared their frustrations with the volunteers who ran the club.

When the issue of selling the property first came up, his initial reaction was: "No." He didn't like the idea of the Deaf community feeling so homeless. Even with the proliferation of ASL classes in high schools and colleges, they were still firmly in the hearing world. They'd always need reprieve from working all day in hearing environments, and that meant time among quality signers.

He didn't tell anyone about the letter. Not at first. He needed to collect his thoughts and figure out how he truly felt about the situation. Later that evening he told his wife, and they talked at length. June loved the Deaf club, too, but she was a pragmatist. There weren't any rich Deaf people in town, and contrary to the community's popular belief about him, Shawn was tuition-poor from paying for his kids' college education. Of course, the city had quite a few hearing people with money, but they were often besieged by the larger nonprofit organizations, but the pity-us-Deaf approach went out of style with peddlers trying to sell manual alphabet cards years ago. Still, the low attendance meant that the interest just wasn't there. He had read the minutes from the board meetings from the last few years; it seemed as if they'd tried everything.

For a long time everyone blamed the ubiquity of mobile technology and social media for the growing dearth of Deaf clubs in America. Then Shawn wondered if the Internet was the newest Deaf club in town. Maybe it was true. No club could possibly hold all the Deaf people in the world, but if the Internet was the world's largest club, there was hope. Online, Deaf people were constantly connecting at all hours; sometimes they argued via video clips posted back and forth. Of course, it wasn't the same thing as those days when Deaf people drove to each other's house just to communicate. Not everyone had TTYs, mail wasn't always quick, and voice relay services did not exist. Everyone appreciated these precious moments together.

But times had become indeed easier for the Deaf. Many hearing people were always surprised to learn of the bitter political undercurrents underwriting the history of Deaf education. As such, they were often receptive to including Deaf people by hiring interpreters. Of course, Shawn knew from his work as a disability rights lawyer, the hearing and able-bodied world had a long way to go in providing accommodation, but the world was indeed a much better place than when the club was first built. He had to seek solace in that fact.

GEORGE WILLIAM VEDITZ
(1861-1937)

Ladies and gentlemen, I float before you. I'm no longer a vision captured on expensive celluloid. Shorn free of my spectacles and suit, I am as real as my hands. For when I died, I was truly happy. I knew in the core of my bones that one day I would arrive at a place like this. Look around yourselves, my dear friends. The walls and windows of this Deaf club may seem simple, Spartan even, but they are ours. When we were human, we toiled hard to raise the funds and built many of these buildings ourselves. Sometimes it felt as if we were building our own churches. Hearing people didn't like us because they saw us as pagans of the worst sort. We didn't use our voices to worship their god of speech. We were oralist failures. We were supposed to become ashamed, but no, we had a singular god greater than their many gods of greed and oppression: our hands. We worship these: the hands we have. Our hands are what makes us feel alive even if the human world considers us dead. Never speaking again feels like an extraordinary gift when you sign freely, as many of us have been doing for decades. I love the looks of joy and relief on their faces when newly released spirits arrive in our midst. They look so confused at first because they'd been raised to believe that when they died, Heaven would be a lofty place aswirl with clouds and cherubs. But we Deaf people are much smarter than that. We've understood that if we fashioned our own Heaven out of Sign, it would feel more like home than anywhere else. These hands are our pearly gates to freedom. Our fingers flutter like angel wings. Our eyes are full of rainbows. The air between all of us is high-octane oxygen, and we're not even up in the clouds! We linger in remodeled remnants of these Deaf clubs because when we were human, we felt safe in these places. We still feel the spirit of community mingling in our invisible veins that we stay connected as in trees whose roots dig deep in the soil and yet reach out to each other that they become gnarly fingers entangled. They pulse to each other their stories and feelings and jokes, and the soil is like oxygen to them. We are also trees but we don't need water to survive. In fact, the only food we need is each other's presence. When you sign, you give off the sweetest fireworks of love. Yes, you might think that a stern-looking old man such as I might look queer using the sign "love," but I meant that in a non-romantic way. We may be a large community but I like to believe that even if we may have an occasional spat or two, we are very much a family. Our arms are wide open for each new Deaf spirit. Many of you have known how I've constantly fought the forces of oralism, and I thank you again for rallying around me, especially against Alexander Graham Bell. He's the perfect example of a person with perfect ears who doesn't know how to listen.

He could also sign, but he chose not to understand us as a language community. Which, if you think about it, is mighty peculiar. If you learn a new spoken language like Hebrew, you can't ignore Jewish culture because it's so embedded in the idioms used. You have to know Jewish culture itself in order to master Hebrew. So how is it that AGB could sign so well and not appreciate us as a people? For we Deaf are indeed a people. Look at how our faces light up when someone starts talking to us. It's as if the rooms of our lives have been dark, and our hands are like matches being struck. We light up. We matter to someone. We aren't an afterthought to our hearing families. Signing requires energy, but together, when we sign, it feels as if we don't need a lot of energy to thrive. Our hands are like the wings of geese flying in a V-formation. The reason why these birds fly that way is because it's efficient for such long distances. Have you noticed how sometimes hearing spirits seem to flicker and fade after ten minutes of conversation? Speech requires a lot of energy because it requires the use of muscles that don't quite exist. Remember how we are mirror surfaces? The larynx doesn't exist at all, so they have to work harder just to speak. What sweet revenge! Have you watched a hearing gathering lately? It's like watching people talking really fast, then fading and resting before starting up again. They're like fireflies! But us in this amazing Deaf club? We are lanterns that never go out of light. Our hands are fire, and we keep each other warm. The hearing world was always a cold place, but the energy contained here in this vast room is beautiful. Look at all of you. Show with your faces how much love—I guess I'm turning into a sentimental old fool after all—you feel toward each other. We've long known that Sign will set us free in a world of no misunderstanding. We don't need to preach this to anyone. We have a very simple rule: We will always love you as long as you worship Sign. Each one of you is a god. When I say "god," I refer not to the Christian nor Greek nor pagan gods. I use the word "god" here because how else can we exalt ourselves and respect ourselves as the amazing creatures that we indeed are when hearing people don't appreciate us at all? For to worship should not have to include fear or oppression. It's easier to do things for someone you love than for someone you fear. A place filled with love is a temple of the highest order. It doesn't need statues. It doesn't need an altar. It doesn't need pews. Our fingers are the sweetest votive candles. When we sign, we pay homage to our Deaf elders, especially our beloved Clerc. My dear Laurent, we don't mean to embarrass you once again with our affection, but what you've done for us is a genuine miracle. You might say that you came to America because of a Deaf girl named Alice Cogswell. If not for you, all of us wouldn't be here. You simply showed us Sign. That most dangerous fact is why proponents of oralism—and hearing parents who still believe deafness to be a calamity—are so fond of implanting babies. If we feel accepted as we are—as in perfectly formed as God has intended us to be—we can truly move mountains. Today I ask for your help. We are gathered here because a group of five Deaf humans has been tasked with deciding what to do with this beloved building. We need to fill their hearts with much love and forgiveness—yes, forgiveness even if they decide to sell. Let us all connect our ghostlights and pray as one for the salvation of this sacred space.

RAYMOND LUCZAK

THE DECISION

Shawn looked at everyone. "Me-feel s-a-d, but ..." he dropped his hands in resignation. "Do-do?"

"Vote," Angela said.

"Hand-raise o-r paper secret?"

"Paper," everyone else signed at once.

Angela took out a sheet of paper, folded it five ways, and tore apart rectangles. "Write Y yes, N no. No names."

A moment later, Rick gathered up the folded strips and swapped them around so no one could tell which one was whose. He showed everyone each response.

The votes came out to three out of five in favor of selling.

Everyone's faces spoke volumes of silence.

Finally, Shawn said, "Me sorry all-this happen."

The fact that Rick, who never cried, had tears trickling down his face was enough.

Shawn tried again. "We can wait later sign-contract."

No one offered to ink their names on the last page.

"Me afraid this will happen. Me prepare d-r-a-f-t letter explain why close." He pulled a printout from his folder.

As each member tried to read the polished draft of the press release with a clear mind, it wasn't easy. They weren't in the mood at all. Finally, they asked Shawn to explain the fine print. One by one, they signed the agreement. He would bring the papers to the Cookson International office on Monday.

Afterward they wandered around the Deaf club as if for the last time, seeing the place as for the first time. They hadn't realized how heavy a heart could weigh in their chests until that day.

In the days and weeks ahead, the former board members would become comforted by the unexpected sights of young Deaf people signing with each other on buses, sidewalks, and airports. As long as Deaf people could find each other, they'd always find a permanent home in the language of understanding what it meant to be misunderstood.

And of course, no Deaf person is ever alone. Ghosts are everywhere.

ABOUT THE AUTHOR

Raymond Luczak lost much of his hearing at the age of eight months and grew up in a hearing family of nine children in a small town in Michigan's Upper Peninsula. He was not allowed to sign until he was 14 years old. He graduated with the legendary Class of '88 from Gallaudet University.

Luczak is the author and editor of over 20 books. Titles include *The Kinda Fella I Am: Stories* and *QDA: A Queer Disability Anthology*. His Deaf gay novel *Men with Their Hands* won first place in the Project: QueerLit Contest 2006. Forthcoming titles include *A Babble of Objects* (Fomite Press) and *Flannelwood* (Red Hen Press). A playwright, he lives in Minneapolis, Minnesota. [raymondluczak.com]

ABOUT HANDTYPE PRESS

Handtype Press was formed in 2007 with the express purpose of publishing select titles of interest to the Deaf and signing communities around the world:

Deaf Lit Extravaganza by John Lee Clark (Editor).

From Heart into Art: Interviews with Deaf and Hard of Hearing Artists and Their Allies by Raymond Luczak.

I Stole You: Stories from the Fae by Kristen Ringman.

Makara: A Novel by Kristen Ringman.

Silence Is a Four-Letter Word: On Art & Deafness (The Tenth Anniversary Edition) by Raymond Luczak.

This Way to the Acorns: Poems (The Tenth Anniversary Edition) by Raymond Luczak.

Through the Tunnel: Becoming DeafBlind by Angie C. Orlando.

Tripping the Tale Fantastic: Weird Fiction by Deaf and Hard of Hearing Writers by Christopher Jon Heuer (Editor).

Where I Stand: On the Signing Community and My DeafBlind Experience by John Lee Clark.

We will always appreciate your purchases of our books at handtype.com. Thank you!

CPSIA information can be obtained
at www.ICGtesting.com
Printed in the USA
FFHW01n0801010818
47528949-50924FF